LOWER THE TRAP

The Lobster Chronicles 1

LOWER THE TRAP

Jessica Scott Kerrin

Illustrations by
Shelagh Armstrong

Kids Can Press

To the Euphemias — J.S.K.

Text © 2012 Jessica Scott Kerrin
Illustrations © 2012 Kids Can Press

Kids Can Press acknowledges the financial support of the Government of Ontario, through the Ontario Media Development Corporation's Ontario Book Initiative; the Ontario Arts Council; the Canada Council for the Arts; and the Government of Canada, through the BPIDP, for our publishing activity.

Published in Canada by
Kids Can Press Ltd.
25 Dockside Drive
Toronto, ON M5A 0B5

Published in the U.S. by
Kids Can Press Ltd.
2250 Military Road
Tonawanda, NY 14150

www.kidscanpress.com

Edited by Sheila Barry
Designed by Marie Bartholomew
Illustrations by Shelagh Armstrong

Manufactured in Shen Zhen, Guang Dong, P.R China, in 10/2011 by Printplus Limited

CM 12 0 9 8 7 6 5 4 3 2 1

Library and Archives Canada Cataloguing in Publication

Kerrin, Jessica Scott
       Lower the trap / written by Jessica Scott Kerrin ; illustrations by Shelagh Armstrong.

For ages 7–10.

ISBN 978-1-55453-576-7

I. Armstrong, Shelagh, 1961– II. Title.

PS8621.E77L69 2012   jC813'.6   C2011-904729-2

Kids Can Press is a *l'©r\S* ™ Entertainment company

Contents

Floater Number Four

"I'll dangle Lynnette by her ankles off the gunwale," Graeme Swinimer swore to himself when he discovered a mummichog floating sideways in his plastic saltwater tub.

Its lifeless, speckled body bobbed above the sand dollars, periwinkles, brittle sea stars, urchins and a rock crab, all part of his marine life collection.

Lynnette was always feeding her food to his fish. What else could explain the soggy banana-and-peanut-butter sandwiches, crusts cut off, hanging in the water?

A dead giveaway.

And this was the fourth floater since the start of the spring lobster season!

Graeme sighed. Ankle dangling would have to wait, because his little sister was at the playground with her buddies from the after-school program. He could hear their screams of glee way off in the distance, along with the *putta-putta* sound of *Homarus II*, his dad's mint-green Cape Islander, motoring home for the day.

Graeme cast about his room for the fishnet. He checked underneath his aquarium magazine, *Cold Marine Tanks*. He skirted past his posters of sharks, whales and sea turtles and scanned the top of his sock-and-underwear dresser. He turned to the other side of his room, which featured a large plaque of sailors' knots mounted next to his closet door.

Aha! There it was, hooked on the knob. He remembered that he had hung the net to dry after

scooping out Floater Number Three just
last week.

Graeme strode across his bedroom's round
braided rug to retrieve the net. Then he dipped
it into the saltwater tub to recover the limp fish.

Down the hall he plodded — *drip, drip, drip* —
into the yellow bathroom with the wicker clothes
hamper that faintly whiffed of lobster and diesel.
Graeme stopped in front of the toilet. *Plop* went
the fish. *Whoosh* went the bowl. Then, as payback,
he grabbed Lynnette's hairbrush and plunged it
deep into the smelly hamper.

Graeme returned to the scene of the crime and
wrote up the incident in his scientific journal. He
included the usual details: the date, the type of
marine animal, the probable cause of death.

Entry completed, he closed his notes,
then gazed into the saltwater tub to observe
the remainder of the school of mummichogs
frolicking between barnacle-covered rocks,

apparently unaware of the recent decrease to their number.

"Graeme's going to be a marine biologist," his dad boasted regularly at the government wharf next to the Lucky Catch Cannery where he unloaded his lobsters.

A longtime widower, Mr. Swinimer was determined that Graeme follow his dream, despite the challenges of having to raise him and Lynnette alone.

"Can't wait!" Graeme always added, riding the wave of his dad's enthusiasm.

The other fishermen would reply by thumping his back good-naturedly with their sausage-fingered hands.

"It'll be nice to finally have a local scientist who knows what's what around here!" they would say.

Fishermen often argued with come-from-away

biologists about the state of the lobster stock in Lower Narrow Spit. But they argued even more with the owner of the town's only cannery about the price for their daily catch.

From the open window above his desk, Graeme heard that the *putta-putta* had slowed down to a dull throb. His dad was maneuvering around the shoals at the entrance to their harbor.

"The sea is as big as the all outdoors," his dad liked to remind Graeme, "but you best mind the rocks in the bay."

Graeme understood what that meant. Even though his dad supported his career choice, he also believed that Graeme should know everything about home port before safely venturing farther away.

Which was true.

Except that Graeme had run out of fresh discoveries. He even knew exactly how many steps it took to get from their white-shingled house to the government wharf where he collected his specimens to study.

For Graeme, the unexplored sea beckoned.

The reverberation of the engine changed again, and Graeme realized that his dad must be getting close to the wharf by now, preparing to throw the lines. When he heard that his dad had cut the engine, Graeme got a move on. He raced past the bathroom and down the stairs, but froze when he heard a knock at the front screen door. A bothersome voice he recognized called out from the covered porch.

"Graeme! You home?"

"Geez Louise," Graeme muttered when he saw who it was.

"Hi, Norris," Graeme said flatly, talking through the screen door, arms crossed. "I was just leaving to meet my dad."

Norris was Graeme's least-favorite classmate.

Unlike the rest of the school, Norris loved dodgeball, and he hammered slow-moving players every chance he got. Norris was always telling everybody what he thought, even when no one asked. He had the annoying habit of jingling coins in his pocket whenever he started to argue, which was all the time. And Norris was the only boy Graeme knew who had the audacity to use the front door rather than the one off the kitchen mudroom.

Norris stared at Graeme with his close-set eyes and smiled with his mouthful of shiny braces. He held a large cardboard box stamped with Lucky Catch Cannery's logo.

Norris's dad was the Lucky Catch's owner, so the logo was a smug reminder of their family's uncommon wealth.

"Know what I've got?" asked Norris in his weasel voice.

Graeme could not help noticing that Norris

had covered his huge forehead with his Big Fish ball cap, a souvenir from one of the biggest aquariums in the world. Norris's family always spent their vacations far away from the campgrounds surrounding Lower Narrow Spit.

Graeme grudgingly pushed open the screen door and stepped onto the porch, careful not to disturb Fetch, his family's gray-muzzled beagle, who spent most of the time impersonating a rug.

Norris set down the box and opened the lid. He reached inside and lifted out a patchy-patterned kitten; one ear black, the other white. The kitten wiggled and struggled about with pitiful mews while Fetch observed the fuss by momentarily lifting his head.

"No wonder you're scratched up," observed Graeme, noting that Norris's arms were covered in angry red marks. "You're holding her all wrong. Here. Let me."

He retrieved the kitten from Norris and

showed him how to cradle her properly. The kitten immediately burrowed into Graeme's chest and began to purr.

"Would you look at that!" Norris said. Then, without missing a beat, he added, "Think you could help me solve an even bigger problem?"

"Depends," said Graeme. He was only half listening, because the kitten was now licking his neck with her pink sandpaper tongue.

"I'm in big trouble," said Norris. "One of Ms. Penfield's cacti is missing."

Graeme looked up. Ms. Penfield was his favorite teacher, and for reasons known only to her, she had assigned Norris, of all students, to take care of her prized plant collection at school while she was off having a baby.

"Missing?" asked Graeme. "Which one?"

"The one with the orange flower on top," said Norris. "I was on the swings after school today, and then I remembered I had to water the plants.

So I came back in, only the cactus wasn't there anymore."

"Ms. Penfield told me that one took *years* to flower," Graeme said. It was a fact that he had made a note of in his scientific journal.

"All I know is that she was planning on entering it at the lobster festival's plant show," Norris lamented. "And now it's gone!"

"Well, there's got to be a logical explanation," said Graeme, rubbing the kitten against his cheek.

Graeme prided himself on applying scientific rules and deductions whenever possible.

"You know what *I* think," said Norris. It was not a question. "I think someone has *stolen* that cactus. Someone who doesn't like me."

Norris dug into his pocket and produced a folded piece of paper, which he handed to Graeme to open.

"Here's my list of suspects."

Fluke

Graeme read the unrealistically short list written in Norris's scrawl. He recognized all the names, even though some were spelled wrong. The kitten tried to bat the list away.

"Why isn't Lynnette on your list?" Graeme asked.

"Lynnette doesn't like me?" Norris replied.

"Not even a little," said Graeme.

"What's *her* problem?" asked Norris. He began to jingle the coins in his pocket.

"You keep pulling her hat down over her eyes whenever you walk by."

"You do that, too!"

"I'm her brother."

"Oh." And then, "So, are you going to help me, or what?"

Jingle, jingle.

"No," said Graeme, handing the list back to Norris with the certainty of the returning tide.

Spending time with Norris would be like pulling up empty lobster traps during the height of the season: a disappointing effort, and unrewarding besides.

"Fine," said Norris with tight lips across his braces. "It's no skin off my nose."

He snatched the kitten from Graeme and stuffed her back in the box. At the same time, there were hollers and cheers down at the government wharf. Both boys stopped to look from the porch railing. An unusually large crowd had gathered by *Homarus II*.

"I wonder what's rattling their socks?" asked Norris in a condescending tone.

"I better get going," said Graeme.

"Yeah, well, I've got things to do, too," said Norris, not to be outdone.

But by the time Norris picked up his box, Graeme had taken full advantage of the distraction and given Norris the slip.

Upon arriving at the government dock, Graeme listened to snippets of conversations as he wove between Goliath-sized fishermen in their black rubber overalls.

"Never seen the likes of it!"

"Must be at least fifty years old!"

"McDermit caught a corker like that in his day!"

Graeme worked his way to the end of the dock. Other brightly painted lobster boats were still motoring in, screeching seagulls in close pursuit, but *Homarus II* was already tied snugly to the wharf's cleats with rope wound in tidy figure eights.

"Hey, Dad!" Graeme called.

His dad, alone on the stern, looked up at Graeme. His crewman, Dexter, was not on board. The air hummed with fish bait.

"Where's Dexter?" Graeme asked, but as soon as his words were out, he gasped.

Hunkered down on the floorboards at his dad's feet was an absolutely gargantuan lobster. It was practically the size of Fetch, and its antennae, which looked like bicycle spokes, were swinging zigzags in the sea breeze.

"You caught *that?!*" Graeme asked above the rising din.

"You bet!" said his dad, a proud grin on his face. "Dexter had to go to the dentist today, but I took a run to check the lines anyway. This one got its claw caught trying to grab an easy dinner from one of the traps. Come aboard and have a closer look."

Graeme scrambled down the wharf's ladder and hopped onto the boat. He made his way to the stern.

"Geez Louise!" exclaimed Graeme, getting down on one knee for closer inspection, but being careful not to get too close. "Look at the size of those claws!"

Out of the water, the giant lobster could barely move under its massive weight, but its armored claws, too big for elastic bands, were bound by electrical tape, just to be safe.

The behemoth stared at Graeme with its black-bead eyes, an incredible specimen indeed!

"It'd make a great trophy for your shed," said Graeme.

In addition to occasionally capturing creatures other than lobsters in his traps —

tunicates, sea cucumbers and, once, a very small flounder, which he gave to Graeme for his saltwater tub — Graeme's dad also filled a shed in the backyard with curious treasures he had dragged up over the years: old, round-bottomed bottles and fragments of china; anchors from pirate ships and a pewter galley spoon with chew marks; an old lead sounding and cannon balls from battles long ago. There was even a fine-toothed comb made out of bone, which Graeme's dad told him old-time sailors used to comb out lice.

A mounted giant lobster would be a nice addition to his collection.

"Fancy catching this in our very own bay," his dad mused.

"It's got to be a fluke," said Graeme, quickly dismissing the idea that there could be anything left of interest in the water so close to his home.

He stood to look beyond the harbor's raggedy entrance to the open choppy sea. Someday, he would be diving out there, exploring the ocean's uncharted floor where he was certain the mysterious giant lobster had wandered in from.

Graeme's dad silently followed his gaze.

"Say, Swinimer! What's that you've got?" a nasal voice called down from the wharf.

Graeme and his dad looked up. It was pasty Edward Fowler, Norris's dad and the cannery's owner. He was wearing a double-breasted suit bought from Dads and Lads, the fanciest men's clothing store in town. His anchor-patterned silk tie had been flipped over his shoulder by the sea breeze. He had narrow-set eyes, just like Norris.

"That's a lobster, Ed," joked one of the fishermen on the wharf. "I guess you're only used to seeing the canned ones on your Sunday picnics."

Graeme understood the jab. Unlike the owner of a cannery, fishermen could never afford to take time off during lobster season.

The other men laughed at the ribbing, but Edward Fowler persisted.

"That'd make a fine trophy for the cannery," he observed, his eyes firmly fixed on the monster lobster.

"The *cannery!*" another fisherman scoffed. "Are you kidding?! Once reporters get wind of this story, I bet there'll be hundreds of offers from all over for this lobster!"

The crowd rumbled in agreement. Edward Fowler shoved his fists in his pockets and jingled the coins inside.

"That lobster should stay in Lower Narrow Spit," he argued, eyes still on the prize. "And I'm prepared to pay to keep it here."

Graeme's dad turned to the cannery owner,

the front of his overalls shimmering with loose fish scales from cutting up the day's bait.

"Tell you what," he announced to the throng of gawkers as he laid his callused hand on Graeme's shoulder. "I think I'll put today's catch up for auction at the lobster festival." He turned to Graeme. "And if I get the highest bid of the evening, I'll spend the prize money by taking my young marine biologist here on a little trip. Maybe to Big Fish Aquarium?"

"Big Fish Aquarium!" Graeme repeated in delight.

Graeme knew that each year, whoever donated the item that attracted the highest bid at the auction would win prize money totaling more than enough for a trip to Big Fish. Then, to add to his excitement, he realized that the town's annual lobster festival was just over a week away!

Norris's dad turned on his heels and stormed

back to the cannery. But Graeme's dad still had to tally the day's catch, so Graeme headed home on his own after hosing down the boat. He bounded up the front stairs, two at a time. Once he got to the covered porch to give Fetch a pat, Graeme stopped short.

Would the giant lobster really attract the top bid so that his dad could claim the prize money? Last year, the builder of a homemade dory received the award after a stunning bidding war took place over his masterpiece.

Graeme stood at the railing and surveyed the town below, where the festival would soon take place. It was quiet now. The only person he could see was Ferguson, another classmate, walking at a mortician's pace along the main street that wove past Graeme's house, with a bat-shaped kite draped over his shoulder.

Graeme was about to call out to Ferguson, but

then he spotted someone else on Main Street. It was Norris, working his way back up to Graeme's front porch.

"Geez Louise," muttered Graeme, feeling something sour inside.

Bait

Graeme's reflex to hide was not quick enough.
Norris, who was no longer carrying a cardboard
box, waved vigorously, and then he scrambled up
the last of the stairs.

"I heard the news!" he puffed. "That's one
huge lobster!"

He adjusted his Big Fish ball cap, which had
again slid down his huge sweaty forehead after his
strenuous climb.

The sight of that coveted cap pushed away
Graeme's nagging doubts. A fresh wave of
possibility hit him.

"My dad's going to auction it off at this year's lobster festival. Then *we'll* be going to Big Fish. Well, that is, if it brings in the highest bid of the evening," explained Graeme, uncertainty creeping into his voice.

Norris's eyes flickered, and Graeme instantly wished that he had not told him anything. Norris used personal information like a weapon.

"You know what *I* think," said Norris, all weasel-like. Norris never waited for an answer. "No one's going to bid on that giant lobster. The meat will be too tough to eat, if you ask me."

"Tough, maybe," said Graeme. "But some people might want it for a trophy. Take your dad, for instance."

Norris's eyes flickered again.

"That's what *I* thought," he said. "But I just talked to my dad at the cannery, and he's only lukewarm about the idea."

"Didn't seem lukewarm down at the wharf," argued Graeme.

"Oh, he's lukewarm all right," Norris announced with authority. The annoying jingling of coins commenced.

Graeme grasped the railing of the porch and looked out over the empty bay. How could he possibly get to Big Fish for a chance to talk to marine biologists in person if he had to rely on some stupid community auction? Lost in his own despair, Graeme was startled when Norris next spoke.

"You know what *I* think. I can talk my dad into bidding really high on your dad's giant lobster."

Graeme turned to Norris, Norris with his scratched-up arms crossed confidently against his chest, Norris with his polished metal smile, Norris who had been to so many more faraway places than Graeme could ever dream of.

Graeme sighed. With Norris, there was always a catch.

"What's the catch?" asked Graeme.

Norris dug into his pocket and produced his list of suspects once again.

"Help me solve the cactus mystery," said Norris, waving the list in front of Graeme's face like bait.

Graeme glanced down at the government wharf. Already the large crowd around *Homarus II* was dispersing. Everyone was going home for the day.

Or maybe, thought Graeme with stomach flutters of panic, they were already losing interest in the monster lobster.

"Deal," Graeme muttered, and he reluctantly took the list from Norris.

Norris beamed as he spun around and bounded down the stairs for home.

Graeme stepped over Fetch and went around back to the mudroom door. Once inside, he slowly unfolded the paper to review the list.

Where to begin? he wondered.

Graeme was still trying to decide whom to investigate first when he went to feed the giant lobster the next day. He peeled off the lid of an old ice-cream bucket and plucked a stinky piece of mackerel from the greasy contents. What a reek! Then he dropped it into the lobster tank at Lower Narrow Spit Community Museum, which was located in the town's vacated train station.

The mega lobster, now housed inside a tank normally used to keep examples of market-sized lobsters, immediately began to twitch its ramrod antennae. Then it homed in on the bait and gobbled dinner up in lickety-split time.

"Great job, Graeme!" said Ms. Carrington, the museum's director, when she stopped by the tank on the way to her office.

She peered over Graeme's shoulder while he dropped another piece of bait into the water.

His dad had asked him to check on the lobster until the auction and make sure it was eating and that the saltwater temperature stayed cool and even. Ms. Carrington already had enough on her plate, what with having to organize the museum's chowder contest as part of the lobster festival and keeping up with the picky demands of Edward Fowler, this year's judge. But she had readily agreed to keep the monster specimen on display until the auction, because it was sure to attract even more visitors to the little museum.

The telephone rang.

"Excuse me," said Ms. Carrington, and she hurried to her office.

Her voice floated back to Graeme as he recorded the feeding in his scientific journal.

"It's probably over fifty years old," he heard her say.

Graeme guessed that she was talking to a reporter about his dad's spectacular catch.

The giant lobster stared at him, expecting another piece of bait.

"That's enough for today," Graeme announced, and he firmly pressed the lid back on the ice-cream bucket.

He did not want to overfeed the crustacean so that it ended up like one of his sideways-floating mummichogs.

Which reminded him: he had not gotten around to dangling Lynnette by her ankles. He would have to get to that soon, because he had noticed in the morning that her favorite frosted cereal had been sprinkled into his saltwater tub.

"Lynnette!" he had shouted upon the discovery.

When he realized that she had already left for school, he marched to her bedroom and stuffed his clammy socks into her miniature teapot, which was surrounded by daintily arranged matching china cups.

The door to the museum creaked open, and in walked Allen, Ms. Carrington's young son. He was lugging his schoolbag, which he flung onto the table that his mom had set up in preparation for the festival's chowder contest.

"Hi, Graeme," said Allen cheerfully.

Graeme turned to smile at Allen.

Allen was on Norris's suspect list.

"What do you have there?" Graeme asked as Allen started to empty the contents of his schoolbag onto the table.

"Homework," said Allen glumly. "Mostly math, and Lynnette got extra. She kept talking in class."

Unlike his sister, who did not appreciate the finer points of addition and subtraction, Graeme was good at math. He realized that he could easily interrogate Allen while assisting with his homework.

"Need any help?" asked Graeme, careful not to appear too eager.

"Sure!" said Allen, sounding entirely unsuspicious.

Graeme pulled up a chair and sat beside him. He quickly scanned the contents of Allen's schoolbag, on high alert for clues, while Allen rummaged about for his math sheets.

"What's this?" asked Graeme, pulling out a painting from the messy pile.

It featured a crude picture of someone marooned on a deserted island with the word "HELP" written in the sand.

"We got new brushes in art class," said Allen. "You like it?"

"It's really good. Is that you all alone on the island?"

"No. It's Norris. I was mad at him when I painted it."

Allen returned to rooting for his math sheets.

"That Norris," said Graeme with sympathy, but his heart was pumping wildly. "What'd he do to you this time?"

"He wouldn't get off the swings."

"So you drew this?"

"Yes. He never lets me have a turn! And my mom wants me to come here to do my homework right after the after-school program, so I can't wait around all day for him to get off. I haven't been on the swings in ages."

"Do you always come straight here?"

"I have to. Mom says. Why?"

"No reason," said Graeme with disappointment.

Obviously, Allen could not have done anything to Ms. Penfield's cactus if he reported to the museum daily as soon as the after-school program was over.

Interrogation concluded, Graeme pushed his chair back and stood to leave.

"Aha! Here are my math sheets!" Allen announced, and he grandly fanned them out before Graeme.

Trapped, Graeme slowly sat back down.

Scabby Elbow

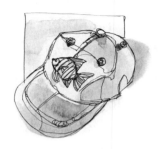

"Hi, Graeme," said Norris, who was waiting on Graeme's front porch for him to return from the museum, all the while picking at a scab on his pointy elbow. "I'm here for my status report."

Norris's annoying habits were relentless: he was still sporting his infuriating Big Fish ball cap! Allen's painting of a marooned castaway quickly came to mind.

"I've just eliminated one suspect," said Graeme, bending down to scratch Fetch.

"Who?" asked Norris.

"Allen Carrington."

"Allen was a long shot," said Norris. He began to snap his fingers, his pet signal for others to get on with it. "You better get cracking on that list. The festival is only a week away. Tasty Foods has already placed their extra-large order at the cannery for frozen lobster."

Graeme surveyed the town below. Soon enough, thousands would descend to participate in the festivities.

There would be the Princess Mermaid and King Neptune Pageant, presented on a temporary stage in the parking lot of the cannery. Lynnette had won the crown last year, a tiara that Ferguson's mother, who ran a bridal gown business called Forever and For Always, had made. Lynnette still flounced around wearing it, even on simple errands like collecting their mail at the post office.

There would be the contest for building lobster

traps, and also the lobster boat races, when all the captains would follow an obstacle course set up in the bay. That always drew huge crowds to the government wharf.

There would be the lobster parade on Main Street, weaving through town and marching right past Graeme's house. Graeme still remembered last year's best float, which was actually not a float at all: an old wooden church that was being moved to a new location had gotten caught in the parade route.

There would be the plant show as well as the crafts fair. Last year's most creative entry was a table lamp made of stacked-up lobster cans built by a resident from Sunset Manor, Lower Narrow Spit's seniors' residence. Graeme had won it as a door prize, and he read his aquarium magazines by it in bed almost every night.

And lastly, there would be the annual lobster

supper and auction, held in the old dance hall next to the small cluster of town buildings: the curling rink, the bank, the drugstore, the post office, the hardware store, the minimart and the diner that sold famous Chinese take-out with a special lobster sauce.

"Don't worry about your list," said Graeme, speaking deliberately to cover the worry in his voice. "I'll get through it in time."

"You know what *I* think," said Norris, not pausing for an answer. "You're worried."

He sat down on the porch rocker and began to creak back and forth.

Creak, creak. Creak, creak.

It was almost as annoying as jingling coins.

Fetch raised his eyebrows at the unpleasant noise, but otherwise did not move.

"Watch Fetch's tail," warned Graeme. "Your rocker's getting awfully close."

"I'm nowhere near Fetch's tail," argued Norris, but he scooted his rocker back just the same. "I'm good with animals, you know."

"I bet," said Graeme dryly. "Say, how's your kitten?"

"What kitten?" asked Norris.

He stopped creaking.

"What *kitten?*" repeated Graeme. "The one you brought over yesterday!"

Norris stared blankly at him.

"In a *cannery box*," said Graeme incredulously.

Could Norris be so spoiled that he had already grown bored by a brand-new pet?

"Oh," said Norris with a yawn. "*That* kitten."

Creak, creak. Creak, creak.

Graeme looked at Norris's arms. The scratch marks were healing, and there were no fresh ones.

"At least you're holding her better."

Norris shrugged.

Graeme studied Norris. His absolute lack of interest was astounding. Unless …

"Did something happen to the kitten?"

"What? No! The kitten's fine," said Norris, but he suddenly returned his attention to his scabby elbow.

"You're sure?" Graeme persisted.

Norris stopped picking.

"Sure, I'm sure. Look, I think we should review my list of suspects," he said in an obvious attempt to change the subject.

"Okay. By the way, you never told me your kitten's name," said Graeme.

"My kitten's name?" repeated Norris, clearly stalling.

"Yes, your kitten's name. Stop stalling."

Creak, creak. Creak, creak.

"The kitten's name is Nails," said Norris at last.

"*Nails?*" said Graeme. He laughed at Norris's lack of basic anatomy. "You named your kitten *Nails?* Kittens have claws, Norris. *People* have nails."

"Well, I didn't name her," snapped Norris. "And enough about the kitten. Let's get to your suspect list, because you're running out of time, if you ask me."

"*Nails!*" repeated Graeme, still chuckling. He pulled the list out of his pocket and scanned it.

"Who's next?" demanded Norris, having another go at his scab.

Georgia was next on Norris's list. She was another of Graeme's classmates, and she often helped out at Tasty Foods, her parents' minimart store.

Graeme grabbed the opportunity to grill her when his dad ran out of cheese that evening during the final stages of making a casserole for their supper. His casseroles always featured a crusty cheese topping.

"This should be enough," said his dad, handing Graeme some money. "A large brick of cheddar will do."

Graeme readily agreed to go, delighted at how easy detective work could be.

"Want to go for a walk?" Graeme called to Fetch on the front porch.

The old beagle shifted to a more comfortable position, but otherwise did not get up.

"That's what I thought," said Graeme, giving Fetch a quick ear rubby before heading down the stairs to Main Street.

"Hi, Violet," said Graeme when he entered the minimart.

Violet, one of Ferguson's endless gaggle of sisters, who were all named after flowers, was a part-time check-out clerk and also sometimes babysat for Lynnette.

"Is Georgia here?" he asked, getting right to the mission at hand.

"She's in the freezer aisle, I think," said Violet as she casually flipped through a teen celebrity magazine while waiting for customers.

Graeme nodded. He marched past the cleaning supplies aisle, the cereal aisle and then the cookie aisle until he reached frozen meats. Sure enough, Georgia was assembling a stand-up cutout of a cartoon lobster next to a freezer bin where the extra-large order of canned lobster would go. The cardboard lobster waved a festival banner featuring the Lucky Catch's logo, and appearing below that, in much smaller letters, were the words "Lower Narrow Spit."

"Hi, Graeme," said Georgia, looking up with a smile. "I hear your dad's lobster is almost as big as this one," she added, pointing to the cutout.

Her lobster looked so comical compared to

the extraordinary specimen he was feeding that Graeme had to laugh.

"Not quite," he said. "But I sure hope it gets the highest bid so that we win the prize money for a trip to Big Fish Aquarium."

"Big Fish Aquarium?" she repeated. "Oh, that's right. You're going to be a marine biologist someday."

"Can't wait!" Graeme said, his standard response. "What about you?"

"Me? I'm going to be a famous chef," Georgia announced.

"That explains your gourmet lunches," said Graeme.

Georgia's lunchbox always featured unusual items: cream cheese and cucumber sandwiches, julienne vegetables with special dips, homemade puddings.

"This year, I'm entering the lobster chowder

contest. I've almost perfected my recipe," said Georgia.

"I hear that Norris's dad is going to be the judge," Graeme said.

Georgia's face clouded over.

"What's wrong?" he asked in alarm.

Crusher Claw

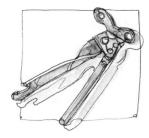

Georgia looked up and down the freezer aisle before answering Graeme under her breath.

"My dad insisted that I go with him to see Norris's dad at the cannery yesterday, when we placed our order for the lobster festival."

"Why's that?"

"Norris has been stealing from my lunches. My dad wanted to have a word with his dad."

"Geez Louise," said Graeme, trying hard to cover up his eagerness at having discovered her possible motive for getting Norris in trouble with the cactus. "How did it go with Norris's dad when you went to see him?"

"He said he'd talk to Norris," said Georgia. "But Norris still took a swipe at my slice of banana cream pie today."

"That Norris," said Graeme, and then, as casually as he could muster, he added, "By the way, what time did you go to the cannery yesterday?"

"I don't know," said Georgia, shrugging. "I came here after school, and then we headed to the cannery."

Graeme frowned. There was no way Georgia could have been involved in the cactus theft. She had been busy working at Tasty Foods during the time that Norris thought the plant had disappeared.

"Are you okay?" asked Georgia.

"Sure," said Graeme, quickly switching gears. "I'm here to buy some cheddar."

"What for?"

"Dad's casserole."

"Come with me."

Georgia led him to the dairy aisle and scooped out a brick of cheese from a refrigerated bin as deftly as Graeme's dad could scoop lobsters out of traps.

"Try this one instead of cheddar," said Georgia. "It will add a nice zing."

"Thanks," said Graeme, already thinking about the next suspect on Norris's list.

Deep in thought, Graeme returned home. Then, during supper, it occurred to him that he might not solve the cactus mystery in time. He could barely enjoy his helping of casserole as he wrestled with *that* unsettling possibility.

The next day, a crowd of visitors watched transfixed as Graeme dropped bait into the mega lobster's tank for its weekend feeding. By now, the crustacean had become a bit of a celebrity. Graeme enjoyed answering questions as it gobbled up its dinner.

"See how its left claw is bigger than its right one?" explained Graeme. "Lobsters start out with same-sized claws, but like people, they figure out which claw they like using better. That claw becomes the larger, crusher claw, and the other one is used for tearing. This lobster's left-handed."

Ms. Carrington poked her way through the crowd.

"Graeme, I have something to show you when you're done."

Graeme pressed the lid back on the ice-cream bucket, then excused himself from the onlookers.

"What's up?" he asked.

She led him into her office and pointed to a yellowed newspaper article that was taped into a dusty scrapbook on her desk. The caption read "Giant Lobster Captured!" The year was 1977.

Graeme peered at the grainy black-and-white photograph in the article. A fisherman was crouched on a wharf beside a mammoth lobster. It must have been the end of the day, because lobster boats were tied up along both sides of the wharf. Graeme recognized the outcrop of rocks at the mouth of the harbor.

"That's *our* government wharf!" he exclaimed.

"Very observant!" said Ms. Carrington. "The fisherman's name was McDermit. He passed away last year, I think."

Graeme quickly read the article.

"It doesn't say what happened to the lobster," Graeme said.

"No, it doesn't. But I don't think it ended up as a trophy. The McDermit family donated a number of interesting items to the museum, like this scrapbook, for instance, but a giant mounted lobster wasn't one of them."

Graeme glanced through the office door and across the museum to the lobster tank. Then he returned to the photograph of McDermit and his giant lobster.

Graeme gasped.

The lobster on the wharf was left-handed! Just like the one his dad had caught!

"Ms. Carrington! What if McDermit returned his lobster to the sea? Do you think it's possible that my dad caught the same lobster again, only years later?"

"No one knows how old a lobster can get," Ms. Carrington said thoughtfully. "Your dad's lobster certainly weighs more than McDermit's. And every time a lobster sheds, it gets bigger and bigger."

"If it isn't trapped," said Graeme, his voice trailing off.

"Well, the only way to know for sure is to find out what happened to McDermit's lobster. McDermit spent his last years at Sunset Manor. He might have made a few friends there who'd know."

Graeme grabbed the magnifying glass on Ms. Carrington's desk. He could make out the names of two of the lobster boats at the wharf.

"*Crack of Dawn* and *Fog Burner*," Graeme read from their sterns out loud. "Maybe the owners of those two boats ended up with McDermit at the seniors' residence."

"How clever, Graeme!" said Ms. Carrington. "Let me make a photocopy of the article for you."

When she left her office, Graeme wandered back to the tank. The giant lobster returned Graeme's stare with its black-bead eyes.

It would be incredible if this was McDermit's lobster, a real scientific link to the past!

But Graeme's next question was troubling: would selling the lobster to the highest bidder be the right thing to do? Maybe, Graeme realized, it should be set free. But if it was, then Graeme's trip to Big Fish would definitely be out of the picture.

"Here you go," said Ms. Carrington, handing him the copy.

Graeme carefully folded the article and tucked it into his pocket, along with Norris's list of suspects.

"When do you think you'll visit Sunset Manor," asked Ms. Carrington, "to chat with some of the residents there?"

"Soon," said Graeme.

Yet, even as he said the word, he was not so sure that he wanted to learn the truth.

Floater Number Five

There was another floater in Graeme's saltwater tub.

Floater Number Five.

And this time, leftover casserole had been dropped into the water. Lynnette had refused to eat her supper the night before, because she hated the zingy cheese topping.

"Lynnette!" Graeme shouted.

No answer.

"Lynnette!" he yelled even louder.

Still no answer.

The only sounds were the whoops and shrieks of kids in the after-school program at the playground and the *putta-putta* of his dad's mint-green lobster boat returning home for the day.

Graeme disposed of the remains with the usual flush and headed straight to Lynnette's bedroom. He slipped all her dresses off their hangers so that her entire wardrobe fell to a crumpled heap on the floor of her closet. As a finishing touch, he tossed her prized tiara, which had been hanging from the closet knob, on top of the angry pile.

He returned to his room and updated his scientific journal about the latest casualty. Then he dug out his copy of the McDermit article and reread it. Even after careful study, there were no new clues about the lobster's whereabouts, and the photo remained frozen in time.

Worry dragged him down like an anchor,

and the air in his room had become suffocating.
A trip to the backyard might help, he decided,
and he headed downstairs.

Graeme pushed through the mudroom door
and wandered across the bumpy lawn to the
clematis vine climbing up his dad's shed. He
counted the budding leaves, then took inventory
of his familiar landscape.

The vegetable garden had just been planted,
and the rhubarb was already up. The remains of
last year's woodpile stood next to half a dozen
lobster traps, stacked neatly and waiting for
repairs. A hammock was tied between two crab
apple trees, where Graeme liked to read about
oceans far away.

He sighed. His surroundings seemed so
cramped and ordinary.

Graeme undid the latch on the shed door
and stepped inside to wrap himself in the cool
shade. While waiting for his eyes to adjust to the

shadows, Graeme took a deep breath: a mixture of linseed oil, diesel and grass clippings.

He gently touched the treasures that his dad had displayed on the shelves: bottles, lead soundings, cannon balls. And above the shelves, the nameplate of his dad's first boat had been mounted: *Homarus,* bought right after he finished high school.

Graeme's survey turned to the floor of the shed. Unlike the tidy shelves, the floor was hidden beneath mounds of fishing nets, ax handles without axes, a three-legged chair, cans of marine paint, tools soaking in coffee cans filled with blackened oil, several broken boat radios, wooden floats, rolled up nautical maps, a rusty teakettle, two cracked hurricane lamps, the lawnmower and an enormous lobster pot too big for their kitchen cupboards, which his dad hauled out each year for the family reunion picnic.

Graeme's eyes rested on the lobster pot.

He knew what he had to do.

"Graeme's going to be a marine biologist."

How often had Graeme heard his dad declare those words? So it was absolutely imperative that Graeme visit Big Fish in person, to make that promise come true.

Graeme would have the means if the giant lobster sold high. All it would take was one keen bidder. One keen bidder whose son was in a pickle about a missing cactus.

Graeme dug out Norris's list of suspects. There were only two more names to investigate. Graeme had a job to do. And he was going to do it.

No matter what headwind blew his way.

On Monday afternoon, Norris planted himself on Graeme's front porch rocker once again, still picking away at his scabby elbow, and still wearing that maddening ball cap. "I'm here for my update," he announced.

Creak, creak. Creak, creak.

Fetch was lying unperturbed nearby in his usual ruglike position.

"Have a look," said Graeme, reaching into his pocket and unfolding the list of suspects. He had crossed off the names of those whom he had already ruled out.

Norris grabbed the list and scanned it, then thrust the paper back to Graeme.

"You know what *I* think?" He did not wait for Graeme to reply. "You're going to run out of time, if you ask me."

Norris began to snap his fingers nonstop.

"What are you talking about?!" Graeme shot back, unable to ignore Norris's exasperating hand signal. "There are only two names left to investigate. And one of them walks by my house all the time."

"Who? Ferguson?"

"Yes, Ferguson. I saw him go by just the other

day," said Graeme, recalling the bat-shaped kite. "Look, here he comes again now."

Both boys watched as Ferguson rounded the corner and passed below Graeme's house, walking at the pace of a funeral march.

"Go on, then," Norris taunted while jingling the coins in his pocket. "Investigate, Mr. Science."

"Don't forget your side of the deal," Graeme warned, and he took off down the stairs. "Ferguson!" he called.

Ferguson stopped to look up. He smiled when he saw that it was Graeme.

"Where are you headed?" Graeme asked as the two set off together.

"I'm going to play table tennis with my granddad," said Ferguson. He patted the paddle that was tucked into his back pocket. "Is that *Norris* on your porch?"

Both boys turned to look back at Graeme's house.

Norris ducked behind the cover of a lilac bush by the front stairs, a beat too late.

"Yes. That's Norris," Graeme admitted.

"I'm dying to know why you're hanging around with *him*," said Ferguson, who resumed walking while Graeme matched his sober stride. "You're not the type who likes cheaters."

"He cheats?" asked Graeme, not at all surprised.

"Constantly," said Ferguson. "He's always trying to copy my answers during spelling tests. I tell him to stop, but, like my granddad says, I might as well flog a dead horse. Norris makes me mad enough to spit feathers."

"Geez Louise!" said Graeme, secretly pleased to discover that Ferguson had a possible motive as a cactus thief.

They walked without comment while Ferguson whistled some kind of solemn church hymn and Graeme plotted his strategy.

"I wonder why Ms. Penfield put him in charge

of her plants," Graeme pondered out loud, cunningly directing the conversation to the crime scene.

"Heaven knows," said Ferguson. "Here's my turn," he added, pointing up a small street that intersected the main one they were on.

But Graeme was not quite done with his investigation.

"I'll keep you company," he offered, and he made the turn with Ferguson.

They walked for a few more blocks. Ferguson mournfully whistled, and Graeme struggled with how to keep the conversation alive.

"Those plants," Graeme finally continued. "They can't be safe with Norris."

"Ms. Penfield was dead wrong to trust him," agreed Ferguson. "Plus, like I said, he cheats."

Ferguson came to a halt. "Well, here I am."

Graeme saw an expansive green lawn sporting cared-for flowerbeds, outdoor furniture arranged in social groupings and old people moving about with canes and walkers. Some of them were watching an elderly man flying a bat-shaped kite that made swooping passes at the onlookers below.

Graeme realized with a jump where they were.

This was Lower Narrow Spit's seniors' residence!

Fog Burner

Graeme tugged at his shirt. His goal was to make sure that the giant lobster got the highest bid possible. That meant he did not want to run into any of McDermit's old fishing buddies at Sunset Manor who would be against putting it up for auction.

"Your grandfather lives *here?*" asked Graeme, his voice cracking.

"That's him with the kite," said Ferguson, pointing.

The kite flyer waved.

"How often do you visit him?" asked Graeme, determined to wrap up his investigation quickly, then make a fast escape.

"Every day," said Ferguson proudly.

"Interesting," said Graeme, but his heart felt like a boat pitchpoling end over end in a stormy sea.

The kite flyer slowly started to walk toward them, tugging the sky-high bat kite along.

"Did you miss any days this past week?"

"No. I always come here straight from school. If it's not ping-pong, then it's Scrabble, or crafts or maybe some outing. Look, there's Mr. Hastings, my granddad's friend. He must have come back from his ear appointment already."

An elderly man wearing a plaid shirt and blue pants hiked up to his armpits nodded at Ferguson from his lawn chair, then ducked from the suicidal kite.

"Ear appointment?" repeated Graeme, disappointment sinking in.

Ferguson could not have been the cactus thief if he had been visiting his grandfather.

"Mr. Hastings is deaf as a doornail," explained Ferguson. "But that doesn't stop him from talking on and on about the boat he used to own. Old fishing stories never die."

Graeme swallowed.

"Do you know what the name of his boat was?" Graeme asked.

He could not help himself. His scientific mind just had to know, no matter how much he struggled against learning the truth.

"Yes," said Ferguson hesitantly. "*Something Dawn.*"

"*Crack of Dawn?*" offered Graeme.

"That's it! *Crack of Dawn.*"

"And your grandfather," Graeme continued

after clearing his throat. "You say he's friends with Mr. Hastings?"

"They were both fishermen," said Ferguson.

"So your grandfather owned a boat, too?"

"Yes. *Fog Burner.*" Ferguson shaded his eyes from the sun to better view the bat with the death wish.

Ferguson's grandfather had almost worked his way to within earshot, bat still swooping manically against the mackerel sky.

"Here he comes now," said Ferguson. "Do you want to meet him?"

Fog Burner. Crack of Dawn. Those were the boats in McDermit's photo!

"Another time," said Graeme, horrified.

He spun around and bolted.

The next day after school, Graeme muttered to himself all the way home. He kept thinking about his narrow escape at the seniors' residence.

Surely it did not matter if his dad had recaptured McDermit's lobster. So there was no point in learning the truth from two old fishermen.

Why, then, was he talking to himself?

Geez Louise!

Graeme paused when he reached the stretch of road below his house. He looked up.

Fetch was comfortably sprawled on the front porch, nose barely sticking out from the top of the stairs. A whirligig on the lawn featuring two men sawing wood moved in the soft breeze. Happily, there was no sign of Norris.

But down at the wharf, someone was talking to Graeme's dad while he was tying up his boat. When Graeme got closer, he could see that the stranger was holding out a microphone.

A reporter!

A reporter from the city, Graeme noted. She was wearing spike-heeled shoes.

"Graeme!" his dad called out jovially. "Come join us!"

Troubling thoughts about Sunset Manor dissolved like salt in water. A reporter was good news. People from all over would read her story about the monster lobster, and that meant more bidders at the auction. More bidders, more money. Big Fish was once again within reach!

"Hello," said the reporter. "I work for the *Daily Story*, and I'm here about your dad's unusual catch."

She thrust the microphone toward Graeme.

"A giant lobster is really big news," Graeme agreed enthusiastically.

"You must be very proud of your father," she said.

"Graeme's been tending it," explained Graeme's dad, wrapping his arm around

Graeme's shoulders. "Did I mention he's going to be a marine biologist?"

"A marine biologist? That's impressive," said the reporter.

"Can't wait!" Graeme said. Then, buoyed by her smile, he added, "Dad's going to take me to Big Fish Aquarium with the prize money if we get the highest bid at the auction."

"*If* there are any bidders," a nasal voice called out from behind them.

Everyone turned.

It was Norris's dad, charging down the wharf from the cannery, his polarized sunglasses reflecting their surprised faces.

"I don't think we've met," said the reporter, turning her microphone to the intruder.

"Surely you've heard of Edward Fowler?" said Norris's dad.

The reporter gave him a blank stare.

"I *own* this cannery," he continued, grandly sweeping his hand in the general direction of the most impressive building in town.

The reporter nodded politely, but turned back to Graeme's dad.

"I'm running a bit behind," she said. "So I only have time for a couple more questions." She held out the microphone. "Where did you catch the giant lobster?"

"Right here in this very bay," said Graeme's dad.

Graeme glanced apologetically at the reporter. He could not understand why his dad was so proud of Lower Narrow Spit, which, as anyone could see, was completely unremarkable.

Boring, even.

Graeme peered around his dad's shoulder, beyond the shoal-riddled entrance, to the open sea.

"And how old do you think your lobster is?" the reporter asked.

Norris's dad wedged himself into the conversation like a sharp pointy fid, a tool fishermen use to separate tight strands of a rope.

"Oh, I suppose it's at least fifty years old. Maybe older," he said authoritatively, while furiously jingling the coins in his pocket.

Graeme's dad winked at Graeme. They both knew that Norris's dad probably got that information by eavesdropping on other fishermen.

Still, Graeme's stomach gave a little heave. The reporter was starting to ask specific questions about the lobster. And this was the *exact* spot where McDermit had been photographed. What if she had done some background research and had read that article, too? Would she make any connection?

Not if Graeme could help it. He scooted over

to the hose on the wharf and started to spray the day's bait off the boat. He hoped that the noise would force the reporter to wrap up the interview quickly and return to the city. Water shot in all directions as the spray hit parts of *Homarus II*, creating a spectacular racket.

"One more question," the reporter persisted, raising her voice after she and Norris's dad leaped away from where Graeme was spraying. "Is this the biggest lobster ever caught in Lower Narrow Spit?"

Graeme panicked. He swung around to the reporter, hose still in hand. She shrieked as the icy cold water sprayed across her skirt and spilled into her fancy city shoes.

"Careful!" warned Graeme's dad. He jumped onto the boat to retrieve a towel.

"Sorry," said Graeme, turning off the hose, cheeks flushed.

"I'm okay," said the reporter, blotting up the water as best she could, while Graeme's dad held her recording equipment. "But I should be going," she added through chattering teeth.

They watched as she made her way down the wharf, squelching water with each high-heeled step.

"Well, I'd better get back to the cannery," said Norris's dad in an uninterested tone. He turned and started down the wharf, silk tie a-flapping.

"See you at the auction," Graeme called out hopefully.

Norris's dad did not answer. He just kept walking.

Dead Ahead

It was feeding time once again, and Graeme dropped greasy bait into the community museum's tank. The mega lobster was doing very well, gobbling up everything that came its way. Flashing cameras did not disturb mealtimes one bit. By now, the crustacean was used to all the attention.

"Interesting story," said a teacher who was accompanying a grade four field trip from a nearby county school. He had finished reading the McDermit article, which Ms. Carrington had posted near the tank. "Whatever happened to that lobster?"

Graeme froze, his hand loaded with bait and suspended over the saltwater tank. The lobster's antennae twitched madly.

"It doesn't say," Graeme replied while struggling to stay calm.

It was all he could do not to snatch the article from the wall and crumple it into a tight ball. What was Ms. Carrington thinking, posting it there for all to read?

The grade fours waited for Graeme to speculate.

Graeme did not oblige.

"Looks like McDermit's lobster was left-handed," observed the same teacher, cutting into the awkward silence. "Like yours," he added, turning to further study the article's photograph.

Graeme's thoughts flew in a thousand different directions. He stood with his mouth open, unable to speak. The bait fell from his hand and plopped into the tank.

Gobble, gobble.

The class clapped their hands in delight, looking to Graeme for more. But Graeme needed a break from the spotlight.

After quickly sealing the ice-cream bucket, he pushed past the group and wandered over to the old cannery equipment display area, where it was much quieter. He had seen this part of the museum many times before, but today something on the wall caught his attention. He moved closer.

It was an oval plaque with a rope wrapped around the outside to serve as a frame. The plaque featured an arrangement of market-sized lobster claws held fast by plaster of paris, each one slightly different from the next.

The plaque had probably been crafted by a cannery worker, thought Graeme. She must have come across lobsters with especially interesting claws, and collected those claws over time, much like the observations that Graeme collected in his journal.

Graeme stood in awe. Here was someone else who found time for scientific study, even while working on a busy cannery processing line!

Curious about who had given this plaque to the museum, Graeme read the small label at the side of the frame.

"Donated by the family of Audrey and Lawrence McDermit," Graeme read out loud.

Lawrence McDermit of the giant lobster fame, Graeme deduced.

And Audrey must have been McDermit's wife.

That thought did not have much time to sink in, because right at that moment, there was a commotion at the museum's front door.

"We're here!" shouted one old man to another as they entered the museum.

"What?" the other old man asked.

Ferguson, who accompanied the two, led the elderly gentlemen inside.

Graeme's heart began to pound in his ears. It was the men from Sunset Manor: Fog Burner and Crack of Dawn!

"Hi, Graeme!" Ferguson called out with delight. "My granddad and Mr. Hastings are here to see your giant lobster!"

"Great," said Graeme weakly, his feet cemented to the floor.

"There it is, dead ahead," said Ferguson, pointing to the tank.

"What?" asked Crack of Dawn, adjusting his hearing aid.

Ferguson led the two men over to the mega lobster. The grade four class split to let the seniors through.

Graeme observed from afar as the scene played out in what seemed to be slow motion. Then he watched in agony when he saw Ferguson's grandfather spot McDermit's article on the wall and say something to the crowd.

"What?" asked Crack of Dawn.

"Hey, Graeme! Come on over," Ferguson called. "My granddad wants to tell you something."

"Sure thing," Graeme called back, trying desperately to sound casual.

It was all he could do to make his legs move one step at a time. And all he could think about was how Ferguson's grandfather would claim that this lobster was McDermit's lobster, how the town would then rally behind the idea of letting the lobster go free, and how there would be no bidding and no Big Fish Aquarium.

"Your lobster's in awful good shape," remarked Fog Burner, when Graeme was within earshot.

"What?" asked Crack of Dawn.

"Thanks," said Graeme, shrinking from all the eager eyes in the crowd.

"I was on the wharf when McDermit caught his lobster," said Fog Burner, pointing his knurly finger at the posted article.

By then, Ms. Carrington had joined the group. She spoke.

"I was wondering. McDermit never donated a mounted giant lobster to the museum. Do you know if he set it free?"

The class fell silent, pondering the possibility. In the distance, a foghorn sounded. Graeme felt like he had been washed out to sea.

"No, he didn't," said Fog Burner matter-of-factly.

Graeme's jaw dropped.

"What happened to it?" asked Ms. Carrington.

"McDermit's lobster died," explained Fog Burner. "Something about the change in water temperature or the salt level in the brine. I can't quite recall."

"It died?" repeated Graeme, finding his voice at last and grabbing onto that life vest of information.

But his relief was short-lived, because the next words spoken swallowed Graeme whole.

"It was McDermit's biggest regret," Fog Burner continued. "McDermit told us that something surviving that long should have been returned to the sea."

The heads in the crowd started to nod, one by one.

"What?" asked Crack of Dawn.

Whale Bone

Graeme was almost out of time. The lobster festival was only days away. And now that the news about McDermit's biggest regret was out, Graeme was certain that everyone would agree with what McDermit had said, and there would be no bidders.

No bidders, except — maybe — Norris's dad.

That slim hope was the only thing left for Graeme to cling to as he reviewed the name of the last classmate on Norris's suspects list: Deckland.

So unwavering was Graeme's determination

that he barely glanced at one of his favorite landmarks as he marched to Deckland's house: a giant bone displayed in a flowerbed in Deckland's front yard. The bone had come from a dead whale that had washed up years ago. After a biologist had visited the site and determined that the whale had died of natural causes, the sun-bleached bones ended up decorating the yards of many Lower Narrow Spit homes.

Graeme knocked on the mudroom door. Deckland's mother answered.

"Why, hello, Graeme! How lovely to see you!"

"Is Deckland home?" Graeme asked, no time for niceties.

"He's in the garage putting the final touches on the float."

Deckland's family owned the Toolbox, the town's hardware store. Each year, the store entered a float in the lobster festival's parade.

They built it in the family's garage. Graeme went around back to check it out.

"Hi, Graeme," said Deckland, who was painting the letters on the float's banner. "What do you think?"

Graeme looked up at an enormous constructed lobster that stood in front of the entrance to a canvas-painted cave. It was waving its two monster claws in the air, grasping a hammer and a drill in each.

"Geez Louise!" exclaimed Graeme. He read the banner out loud. "Hardware for your lair. Oh, I get it! That's funny."

"My dad's quite the poet," said Deckland, painting the last letter with finesse.

"You're doing an excellent job," Graeme said, easing into his final interrogation.

"It's these new brushes," said Deckland. "Dad donated a bunch to the school. The trick is, you have to clean them properly, or they'll go all hard and crusty."

He walked over to the utility sink and turned on the water to demonstrate.

Graeme recalled Allen's painting and the new brush he had used to maroon Norris on a desolate island. Thinking of Allen also reminded Graeme of the antics on the swings that had inspired that painting.

"Say," said Graeme as casually as he could muster. "Weren't you the after-school playground monitor this past week?"

Graeme realized with a thrill that Deckland's volunteerism meant he had easy access to the cactus.

"You bet," said Deckland. "And it'd be a whole lot easier if some people would learn to take turns."

"Like who?" asked Graeme, even though he already knew the answer.

"Like Norris," said Deckland. "He thinks he owns the swings."

Thump!

A patchy-patterned black and white kitten jumped down to the sink from the rafters.

"Nails!" exclaimed Deckland. "You crazy kitten!"

"Nails?" repeated Graeme.

Graeme was sure that this was the same kitten Norris had brought to Graeme's front porch in a cannery box.

"What's Norris's cat doing here?" asked Graeme.

"This isn't Norris's cat," said Deckland, scratching behind Nails's ears. "Nails is mine."

The kitten began to purr up a storm.

"*Your* cat!" said Graeme. "Well, that makes sense. Nails is a great name if your family owns a hardware store."

Graeme stood puzzled. Norris had tried to

trick him about the kitten. That meant his list of suspects was probably bogus, too. Graeme started to wonder whether *anyone* on Norris's list had *anything* to do with the missing cactus.

"What's wrong?" asked Deckland.

"Take a look," said Graeme, and he produced the list with Deckland's name on it, written in messy writing.

"What's my misspelled name doing here?" Deckland asked.

"Norris told me someone on this list stole Ms. Penfield's cactus. The one with the orange flower on top."

Deckland frowned. He took a step back.

"Are you saying you think I stole?"

"No!" said Graeme, cheeks flushed. "Of course not!"

"But you're here!" said Deckland. "You're asking me questions! You're *investigating!*"

"Well, yes," said Graeme, sheepishly. "But don't you see? I was tricked!"

Deckland stared at Graeme. Then he turned to the sink and started scrubbing his brushes with such viciousness that Graeme quickly stuffed Norris's nasty list back into his pocket.

"I've got things to do," said Deckland, not looking up.

"Listen! I'm sorry!" Graeme pleaded.

Deckland kept scrubbing.

Graeme stood for an excruciating minute longer, then quietly slunk out of the garage. Once he slipped by the whale bone, he picked up his pace and fled for home.

Norris was waiting on the front porch.

"Why'd you trick me?!" demanded Graeme as he sprang up the stairs two at a time.

"What do you mean?" asked Norris, all weasel-like.

"Nails isn't your kitten! And no one on your list stole Ms. Penfield's cactus!"

Norris smiled, his braces glinting in the sun.

"See! Everyone says you're smart! That's why I picked you," said Norris.

He sat down on the rocker.

Creak, creak. Creak, creak.

Graeme remained standing, fists clenched, shoulders pressed to his ears. Norris stopped rocking.

"Look. I accidentally knocked the cactus to the floor," Norris explained without remorse. "I tried to catch it as it fell, but it scratched me up before the flower broke off, so I had to toss the whole thing into the compost bin. I thought that if I got you to do some investigating, others might be suspected of causing its disappearance, and then I'd get off the hook. The kitten was a nice decoy, you have to admit."

Creak, creak. Creak, creak.

Graeme's stomach felt like one of the knots from his sailors' wall plaque. He opened his mouth, but the words jammed in his throat. He had been duped!

Duped!

"And it worked!" Norris stood. "Because of you, there'll be plenty of accusations cast about. So don't worry. You've done your part. Now all I've got to do is talk my dad into bidding high on your giant lobster."

Graeme did not wait for Norris to leave. Cheeks flaming with humiliation, he stepped over Fetch, heaved open the front screen door and let it slam shut behind him. Then he wheeled around to make sure that Norris had not dared to follow him.

But Norris had been blocked. Fetch, having risen to all fours, now stood staring at him without a single wag of his tail.

Cold Puddle

It was not long before everyone on Norris's list found out about Graeme's hurtful investigation, and he was confronted over and over.

"When did *you* get so sneaky?"

"How am I supposed to trust *you* ever again?"

"I thought *you* were smarter than that."

For once, Graeme had no answers. Instead, he sat alone at recess, listlessly turning the pages of *Cold Marine Tanks*. Clearly, he was not as clever as he thought he was. And now everybody in Lower Narrow Spit knew that, too.

Graeme hung his head.

It did not help that Norris kept insisting his dad would bid high on the giant lobster.

"You know what *I* think," he told Graeme on his way to the playground. "You're mad at me now, but after you spend the prize money at Big Fish Aquarium, you'll forget all about it, if you ask me."

Graeme seethed. How would he, or anyone else for that matter, forget about the whole sorry mess once the giant lobster was permanently mounted as a trophy in the Lucky Catch Cannery for the entire community to witness?

That bitter realization plagued Graeme all day long.

When the end-of-school bell rang and Graeme escaped for home, he saw that there were no new floaters in his saltwater tub. But even that gave him precious little satisfaction.

Graeme sat, head in hands, and tried to organize his jagged thoughts. He could not let

Norris's dad win the lobster. That was for certain. Yet he desperately wanted to go on his trip. So there would have to be another bidder.

But who?

Think. *Think!*

Then it hit him like a tidal wave.

There was another logical bidder for the giant lobster. Of course!

Big Fish Aquarium!

Graeme dashed downstairs to the kitchen. He picked up the telephone, which was on the counter next to a trail of bread crumbs and a half-licked knife with strawberry jam on it. Would Lynnette ever learn to clean up her messes?

"Hello, Operator?" said Graeme after dialing Information. "Would you please put me through to Big Fish Aquarium?"

Graeme listened to the rings while his heart pounded in his chest like the diesel engine on *Homarus II* fighting gale-force winds. Then he stepped into a cold puddle. Lynnette must have knocked over Fetch's water dish in her haste. Geez Louise!

"Good afternoon. This is Big Fish Aquarium. How can I help you?"

"May I please speak to the chief marine biologist?" asked Graeme, using his best telephone etiquette while hopping on one foot and peeling off his wet sock.

"Certainly."

As Graeme listened to the *beep-beep* sounds, he grabbed Lynnette's Raggedy Ann doll from a kitchen chair and used her to mop up the floor with his foot. And then:

"Richard Zwicker speaking."

"Are you the chief marine biologist?" asked Graeme, standing bolt upright.

"That's me," said an amused voice.

Graeme took a deep, steadying breath.

"My name is Graeme Swinimer, and my dad

caught a giant lobster. It's in a tank at the Lower Narrow Spit Community Museum. It'll be put up for sale at the lobster festival auction this weekend, and I think your aquarium might want to buy it."

"Right! I read about your lobster in the *Daily Story*. It's an amazing catch."

"So do you think you'll come and bid?"

"Let me ask you this. Is it healthy?"

"You bet," said Graeme. "I've been feeding it and watching the water temperature and salt level, and recording everything in my scientific journal."

"Interesting," said the marine biologist. There was a thoughtful pause. "I'll have to check with my director, but I think your giant lobster might make a fine specimen for our tank on northern waters. And I'd love to get out for a dive. The last time I was in your bay was years ago, because a dead finback had washed ashore."

"Our neighbors have one of those bones in

their garden," said Graeme. "And my dad can take you out on his boat," he added, grasping for anything that might clinch the deal. "He's a lobster fisherman."

"Okay, then! I'll see what I can do."

When Graeme hung up, his hand was shaking, although he could not tell if it was from excitement or relief or the promise of revenge.

As soon as Graeme's dad came through the mudroom door, Graeme told him about his well-timed call to Big Fish.

"And I talked to a real marine biologist," explained Graeme proudly. "I think he's going to come and bid."

"That's good news," said Graeme's dad. "A bidding war will bring in more money for the community as well as earn us the prize for our trip!"

He yanked off his rubber boots, then went into the kitchen to wash his hands before starting supper. While he splashed at the sink, he added, "Looks like it's clear sailing to Big Fish from here on in!"

Reassured by his dad's optimism, Graeme stood at the living room window and watched the tide turn. He reached out his hand with such confidence, he could almost touch the mouth of the harbor that led to the seascape beyond.

That confidence was not misplaced. Sure enough, Richard Zwicker stopped by the community museum on the day of the auction, just as Graeme pressed the lid back on the ice-cream bucket.

"This is a fine specimen, Graeme," he remarked as he stood in front of the giant lobster's tank. "Be sure to save me a seat for the bidding."

Then he set off with Ms. Carrington to view the remaining displays.

The rest of the day was a sleepwalk. Graeme

barely took in any of the festival's events: the lobster boat races, the parade, the chowder contest.

Only the Princess Mermaid and King Neptune Pageant managed to wake him up. When the time came for Lynnette to step forward to give up her crown to the next princess recipient, she instead grabbed the lobster cape that Ferguson's mom had made for the occasion and bolted from the stage in hysterics.

"I'll catch up with you at the supper," his dad called to Graeme in the crowd as he headed after Lynnette.

The community supper of boiled lobsters, potato salad and blueberry buckle sold out, and, once fed, everyone rushed to the chairs that had been lined up in the old dance hall for the auction. Graeme managed to grab three seats that were only a few rows back from the front podium.

His dad sat on one side; Big Fish's chief marine biologist sat on the other; and Lynnette sat at home, grounded, with her babysitter, Violet, for company.

Now Graeme was on full alert. He surveyed the room to see who else was in the audience while several reporters and camera operators stood along the aisle, recording the whole event.

Norris and Norris's dad were plunked down front and center. Right behind them was Ms. Carrington, sporting a museum polo shirt, and her son, Allen. Allen had rolled up the auction program to fire spitballs at the back of Norris's head whenever Ms. Carrington was not looking.

Nearby was Ms. Penfield, showing off her new plump-cheeked baby to Ferguson's gushing sisters. During the supper, Graeme was not pleased to overhear his teacher tell Norris that she now had something far more important to look after than her cactus, so not to worry. But Graeme quickly forgave her for not being harder on Norris when she later passed Graeme on the way to the dessert table. She said that she would keep her fingers crossed to bring Graeme luck during the bidding.

On the opposite side of the room, Graeme spotted Ferguson busily chatting with a row full of seniors from Sunset Manor, along with Ferguson's grandfather and his friend Mr. Hastings.

And then there were Graeme's other classmates, including the rest who had made Norris's list, scattered throughout the audience and still glowering at Graeme whenever he looked their way.

Surrounding the podium, various items to be auctioned off were on display: a free membership to the curling rink, a crate of canned lobster packed on ice, knitted fisherman's sweaters, a gift basket from the drugstore, a voucher for lunch for two at the Chinese restaurant, gardening tools, homemade pies, and crafts made by residents at Sunset Manor. And, of course, taking center stage, the monster lobster stared out from its tank.

The town's postmaster and volunteer auctioneer stood at the podium. The town's mayor stood behind him to assist with the bidding.

A hush filled the room. Graeme's mouth went dry.

Lucky Catch

"Good evening and welcome," boomed the auctioneer. "Let's waste no time and get straight to the bidding. First up, a crate of the finest canned lobster in the world, generously donated by Lower Narrow Spit's very own cannery."

"That's Lucky Catch," Norris's dad added. He half stood and waved to the crowd. Graeme noticed that the tops of Norris's ears went pink at the muted response from the audience.

"Now, who wants to start the opening bid?" asked the auctioneer cheerfully in an effort to end the awkward silence.

Graeme leaned over to his dad.

"When will the giant lobster be auctioned?"

"Probably not until the very end. It's what everyone has come to see. The auctioneer will want to build the suspense."

"Geez Louise," Graeme grumbled.

He tugged at his shirt, which was sticking to him.

"Hey, bada-bada-bada," called the auctioneer as bids started to roll in.

The auction went on and on, one item of inconsequence selling after another. Slowly, slowly the stage grew bare around the behemoth.

And then there was just one item left, displayed like a gargantuan centerpiece on an empty dining room table.

"Well, ladies and gentlemen. That concludes Lower Narrow Spit's annual lobster auction. We've got nothing left to sell ... no, wait. What's this?" joked the auctioneer, turning to the giant lobster in mock amazement.

The crowd laughed at his antics.

Graeme did not think he was funny.

"Do I have an opening bid?" asked the auctioneer.

Norris's dad confidently held up his paddle and nodded to the cameras.

"Hey, bada-bada-bada," droned the auctioneer. "Hey, bada-bada-bada."

Graeme elbowed Richard Zwicker. The Big Fish biologist put up his paddle, too.

"We have a second bidder!" announced the auctioneer with a mix of surprise and delight.

Both Norris and his dad spun around to see who would dare outbid them. They did not recognize the stranger sitting beside Graeme.

Graeme beamed.

"Hey, bada-bada-bada," called the auctioneer. "Hey, bada-bada-bada."

Norris's dad rammed his paddle into the air.

"Hey, bada-bada-bada. Hey, bada-bada-bada."

The marine biologist shot his paddle up in retaliation.

"Hey, bada-bada-bada. Hey, bada-bada-bada."

Back and forth. Back and forth. The bids getting higher and higher. The back of Norris's dad's neck growing the color of boiled lobster.

Then Norris's dad shouted to the auctioneer. "Let's put an end to this silliness! I'll give you *double* what the last bidder gave!"

The crowd gasped.

Graeme's dad whispered to Graeme. "That's the highest bid of the night! I think we've just won the prize money for our trip!"

But his words were cold comfort. Graeme was desperate for Norris and his dad not to win.

"Bid again," Graeme urged Richard Zwicker. "I'm sure you can outbid them."

The marine biologist hesitated, then signaled to the auctioneer that he was still in the game.

But Graeme noticed that his paddle was shaking.

The crowd leaned forward in their seats. All eyes turned to Norris's dad.

Norris's dad sat staring straight ahead. Norris looked up at his dad, then back at the stranger bidding against them, then to his dad once more.

Nobody breathed, especially Graeme, who felt as if his lungs would soon burst.

"Hey, bada-bada-bada. Hey, bada-bada-bada."

Norris's dad slowly raised his paddle, electrifying the crowd.

Everyone shifted in their seats, then turned to the marine biologist.

But the Big Fish biologist did nothing. Instead, he slumped his shoulders and laid his paddle on his lap.

"It's your turn to bid," Graeme whispered, sweat beading on his forehead.

"Sorry. That was as high as I'm allowed to go."

"This can't be over!" Graeme pleaded.

But when Richard Zwicker would not meet his eyes, Graeme understood the awful truth.

Graeme put his head in his hands.

"Now hold your horses! That lobster's not sold yet!" a new voice shouted from the crowd. "It's our turn to join the bidding!"

Graeme dared to look up. It was Ferguson's grandfather, Fog Burner, surrounded by his Sunset Manor cronies, along with Ferguson, who was grinning from ear to ear. The old man clutched a paddle in his big-knuckled fist and thrust it into the air. The reporters and camera operators adjusted their equipment to record the thrilling turn of events.

"Something that's survived so long deserves to be set free," announced Fog Burner, speaking directly to the cameras. "That's what McDermit always told us."

"So we've pooled our money, and we're going to bid in his memory!" Ferguson added, waving a wad of money in the air as proof.

The audience murmured their approval. Graeme wiped his palms on his pants.

The auctioneer started up again.

"Hey, bada-bada-bada. Hey, bada-bada-bada."

Norris's dad kept his back to the audience when he raised his paddle and nodded deliberately at the auctioneer.

The audience muttered unhappily.

"Hey, bada-bada-bada. Hey, bada-bada-bada."

Ferguson's grandfather jabbed the air with his paddle.

The audience whooped and stomped their feet.

"Hey, bada-bada-bada. Hey, bada-bada-bada."

Norris's dad responded with his paddle, held up defiantly for all to see.

The crowd made grumpy noises.

"Hey, bada-bada-bada. Hey, bada-bada-bada," said the auctioneer, tugging at his collar.

Graeme fought the urge to run up to Norris's

dad and jettison his paddle out the window. He looked over to Ferguson's grandfather.

The old man was now in a huddle with his buddies and Ferguson, who looked very grim, indeed. The huddle cleared, then Ferguson's grandfather raised his paddle again. Only this time, he seemed as if he was looking defeat in the eye, as if this was the last bid that Sunset Manor could manage.

The audience saw that look.

Norris's dad saw that look, too. He turned back to the auctioneer with an arrogant smile and jingled the coins in his pocket with his free hand. Then he raised his paddle one last time with the confidence of the owner who ran the town's only cannery.

"Hey, bada-bada-bada," said the auctioneer, mustering no enthusiasm whatsoever.

Ferguson's grandfather shook his empty fist in the air, muttered a curse, then sat down. The other seniors reached over from their chairs to thump his back in sympathy. Ferguson gave him a hug.

"Sold to the highest bidder," announced the auctioneer flatly. "I'm sure this giant lobster will make a fine trophy for the cannery, to be enjoyed by the folks of Lower Narrow Spit for years and years to come."

Graeme could tell that, like him, the audience was struggling not to lose their manners completely.

"I won!" exclaimed Norris's dad.

A smidgen of applause flittered across the room.

Norris's dad stood and cleared his throat. He began making his way to the podium to say a few words, having paid a princely sum for his trophy.

And then something unexpected happened.

Norris bolted from his chair and scooted past his dad to the podium. He quickly bent the microphone down to his height.

Graeme sank into his seat. What was Norris up to? What new humiliation was he about to heap on Graeme for the entire town to witness?

"I want everyone to know," announced Norris, rushing his words, "that my dad has decided to set the giant lobster free!"

Norris's dad froze in mid-stride. He sputtered, and his mouth stuck half open. It was clear that he had promised nothing of the sort.

Graeme looked at Norris in disbelief. But Norris signaled Graeme with snapping fingers: get on with it!

Graeme seized the moment.

"Hear, hear!" he exclaimed to the stunned audience. He jumped to his feet and began to clap.

From across the room, Ferguson hesitated briefly, a beat behind Graeme. But when Ferguson stood and clapped, the crowd roared their applause and joined the standing ovation.

Norris's dad turned to the audience. His furious look gave way to surprise, then to a flattered smile. Norris stepped away from the microphone to make room for his dad at the podium. His dad grabbed Norris's hand, and the two faced the cheering crowd, arms held up in victory.

Lower Narrow Spit

The darkness in Graeme's bedroom was the color of the monster lobster's black-bead eyes when the alarm clock shattered the silence, startling Graeme awake. Stars shone in unfamiliar patterns through his window. And the only sound he could make out was the air bubbler for his saltwater tub.

A soft knock came on the door. Graeme's dad stuck his head in, along with a beam of light that swept the room and made Graeme's eyes squeeze shut against it.

"Porridge is ready," his dad said.

"Okay," Graeme said groggily. "I'll be right down."

Graeme turned on the lamp made of lobster cans next to his bed and snuggled back into the warmth of his flannel sheets while listening to his dad trundle down the stairs.

Then he took a deep breath, whooshed back his bedding and jumped onto the round braided rug. He scrambled to the bathroom and ran some warm water to wash his face.

As he walked back, he passed Lynnette's room. Her rainbows-and-fairies-patterned bed was empty. After witnessing Lynnette's onstage meltdown, Ferguson's mom had offered to sew her a Former Princess Mermaid cape to wear for keeps, and Violet had taken her back home for a sleepover so that Lynnette could watch the cape being made.

Graeme pulled on the chilly clothes that he

had worn at yesterday's auction and added another sweater plus thick wool socks. Rubbing his arms, he made his way downstairs to the light in the kitchen. His dad was at the stove. The smell of coffee brewing filled the room. Two lunchboxes sat on the counter, packed and ready to go. And Fetch, who had wandered in and taken an obligatory drink from his water bowl, looked at both of them with sleepy red eyes, then slunk back to his own cozy bed.

Graeme glanced out the window above the sink. It was still dark out, only less so. He could make out the silhouette of his dad's shed of treasures in the backyard. He sat down to a bowl of steaming porridge sprinkled with brown sugar while his dad poured him a glass of orange juice.

The two did not say a word as they ate. It would have broken the magical quiet that was all around.

Graeme's dad pointed to the ship clock on the wall: time to go. Graeme scooped the last bit of porridge, then took the bowls and rinsed them at the sink while his dad retrieved their floater coats and rubber boots in the mudroom.

Outside, the world was brighter, but there was still no sun. The black-roofed houses of Lower Narrow Spit slept on as Graeme and his dad made their way down to the government wharf.

Graeme spotted a figure standing by *Homarus II*. It was Richard Zwicker, along with his pile of scuba gear.

"A dive will be just the thing!" the marine biologist declared with excitement.

Farther down on the wharf, inspecting all the lobster boats, were Ferguson, Ferguson's grandfather and his buddy Mr. Hastings. They joined the group when Graeme and his dad arrived.

"Top of the morning," said Fog Burner jovially.

"What?" asked Crack of Dawn, adjusting his hearing aid.

Ferguson nodded curtly, having not yet forgiven Graeme. But Graeme hoped that Ferguson would change his mind if all went well on the outing that they were about to take.

Graeme's dad climbed down the ladder to the boat and started the engine.

Puffs of diesel wafted across the inky surface of the water. There was hardly a ripple.

"If we head out soon," Graeme's dad announced, switching on the navigation equipment, "the tide will still be with us."

Graeme scrambled down the ladder, followed by the others. Everyone found a spot to sit on the stern as Graeme handed out the life vests.

"How's our special guest?" Fog Burner asked.

Graeme lifted the lid off the water tank in the

hold. The giant lobster twitched its spokelike antennae.

"Good to go," said Graeme, replacing the lid.

The mega lobster had been moved right after yesterday's auction to spend its last night of captivity on the boat.

"You weren't going to leave without us, were you, Swinimer?" a nasal voice called down from the wharf.

Everyone looked up. It was Norris's dad with Norris close in tow. They were loaded down with camera equipment and wearing full survival suits and tourist-yellow sou'westers, even though there was not a cloud in the sky.

"Just warming up the boat," said Graeme's dad, looking like he was trying hard not to smile at their silly gear. "Climb aboard."

"You know what *I* think," said Norris's dad when they settled in the stern. He did not wait for an answer. "My release of this lobster will make a splendid photograph for the cannery."

The passengers nodded amicably.

"What?" asked Crack of Dawn.

And then the sun peeked above the horizon.

"Would you look at that!" Norris exclaimed as pinks and oranges burned across the sky.

"Haven't you ever seen the sunrise from a boat?" Graeme asked, pushing the stern off the wharf with the gaffing pole after *Homarus II* dropped her lines.

"No," Norris said proudly. "Dad says there's no need. I'm going to run the cannery when I grow up."

Norris turned away from the receding silhouette of Lower Narrow Spit and snapped a photograph of himself with the entire town behind him.

"Your dad tells me you're going to be a marine

biologist," said Fog Burner, thumping Graeme on his back.

For once, Graeme did not answer, "Can't wait."

Instead, he turned to survey the passengers on board, an unlikely assembly of Lower Narrow Spit residents, each one having navigated past all kinds of obstacles to be there; each one worth knowing better.

Graeme returned his attention to Fog Burner. "Someday," he replied.

Then Graeme joined his dad at the helm as *Homarus II* slid past the crop of rocks that marked the raggedy mouth of their harbor.

Acknowledgments

The generosity of Nova Scotians is legendary, and the time Gussy Rhyno took me out on his lobster boat in Sambro Harbour for some beginner lobster-hauling lessons was no exception. The gray-palette day featured fog mixed with drizzle. Many of the pots came up empty — he referred to this as "changing the water in the traps." And we ended up tossing most of the lobsters we did catch — or "bugs" as he liked to call them — back into the sea. They were either too small or were "berried" females carrying thousands of eggs. I am fascinated by our relationship with creatures we eat. At times, Gus yanked snapping lobsters out of their traps, none too gently, and chucked partially chewed-up fish heads that he used as bait into a waste bucket (occasionally missing and hitting me in the leg instead); at other times, he carefully lowered errant little crabs he had captured back into the water, but then later, gathered up a few of them to crush under the heel of his no-nonsense rubber boot and use as bait for the final traps when he ran out of fish heads.

Gus had a job to do, and he loved his work, much like Graeme's dad.

I also want to thank staff employed on various floors of the Museum of Natural History in Halifax, and who advised me about lobsters and the lobster communities they knew: Victoria Castle, Andrew Hebda, Mary MacDonald and Daniel MacDonald. Paul Collins's boundless passion for rural museums provided an endless source for story ideas. And, Michelle Davey, the manager of the Northumberland Fisheries Museum in Pictou, proved inspirational, because of her love of all artifacts related to fishing.

Finally, I would like to thank my wonderfully supportive editor, Sheila Barry, a lighthouse beacon of guidance and former townie from Newfoundland; Pam Young, who helps run our household and who, among many things, fished lobster for over a decade; and my husband, Peter, who always buoys my spirit and who also makes exceptional lobster bisque.